NOW

Is Once Upon a Time

NOW
Is Once Upon a Time

CAROL TROESTLER

ISBN 978-0-615-26228-4
Published by Golden Footprints Press
Contact: ctroestl@merr.com

Foreword

The author loves to write, sometimes just because a story is waiting to be told. The stories here were written over a number of years. Some were written about things happening in the author's life, and some were stories written from imagination alone. They are dedicated to those who believe in magic wands, castles in the air, and angelic guides who come and help when we need them the most.

NOW is Once Upon a Time

The Path 1

The Magic Carpet 7

The Story of the Golden Footprints........................15

Michael and the Dragons 21

The Moosehunter 25

The Red Convertible 33

The Story of Julia 37

©2008 Susie Anderson

The Path

Once upon a time, a young woman named Sarena decided to go for a walk in the forest near her village. She often walked in the forest, but this day she went deeper into the forest than she had ever gone before. She found herself walking and thinking, and then walking and smelling the fresh air smells of the forest around her.

She took in the aroma of the pine needles beneath her feet, the fragrance of the dampness as she crossed the stream, and she even began to notice how the rays of the sun shown through the trees to the forest floor as if trying to point out special places to her. She listened and sometimes could hear the sounds of little animals, of leaves rustling in the breeze, of her own footsteps on the ground.

Today Sarena was lost in time and did not realize how long she had been in the forest, until the rays of the sun disappeared and the forest began to get dark and cold.

It had been a peaceful and different day for Sarena. She owned a shop at the edge of the village where she sold cloth that she had woven. The cloth was very beautiful with wonderful colored designs. Many people came to her shop with requests for cloth for clothing, cloth for curtains, cloth for coverings for their floors. They found Sarena to be someone who always listened to their needs and tried to fill them.

But this day Sarena had felt that she did not want to weave her cloth or listen to the needs of others. Sometimes she felt that she had nothing more to give.

So this day Sarena had closed her shop and gone into the forest. She had greatly enjoyed her day, but while she had gotten lost in her thoughts and observations, she had also gotten lost in the forest. She decided she had to stop just following where her feet took her. The wind began to blow gently through her curly hair.

"So how am I supposed to find my way out of this forest?" she asked aloud, although there was no other person there. It had been a long time since she had gone an entire day without hearing the sound of her voice, without people talking to her and asking her questions and telling her about their lives, about their dreams, about their problems; their weaving their own tales for her as she wove their cloth for them, and her trying to help them find answers to their problems and feeling like she needed to make them happy.

"I think I know the answer to your question," came a voice that seemed to be carried on the wind. It was wispy and gentle and soft like the breath of a child.

"Where are you? Who is speaking?" asked Sarena. Even though these happenings were strange, she was not frightened.

"You know the way, Sarena," said the voice.

Sarena was beginning to be angry. All her life people had given her directions. She had gotten the directions for weaving her cloth from a great teacher. Even her customers gave her directions on how to weave cloth for them. But now she did not have directions on how to return home. She did not have a map.

Suddenly the wind died down. All around her was silence. She thought that perhaps she had made a mistake in going into the forest.

Her day had been so beautiful and restful and peaceful. But now her feelings towards the day had changed. Right now she longed for the familiarity of her cottage; its wood floor, its strong wooden tables and chairs, her loom and the many colors of her yarn for weaving. She wished that her dog, Samson, was close by wagging his tail and sniffing and chasing rabbits that he would think must be close by. She began to worry about Samson and whether he was thirsty or hungry. She began to worry about her customers and felt guilty that she had not stayed to weave their cloth and had been selfish in going away for the day.

Soon a new breeze began. This breeze made her hair and her long skirt twist around her body. The leaves on the floor of the forest were lifted into the air and swirled and then settled back to the forest floor.

"It is all right, Sarena. It is all right for you to have gone into the forest alone for the day," said a low, strong voice, as its sound seemed to revolve and swirl around her.

"Now who is talking to me?" asked Sarena somewhat impatiently.

"It has been a beautiful day. I'm very glad you are here. No one has ever come this way before. This is your path and yours alone, Sarena."

"But look where it has led me. It has led me nowhere. Now I am lost. My path has gotten me lost and now I cannot find my way back to where I started, back to my home."

She felt torn between her feelings of loss and guilt and her own peacefulness, her aloneness. Somehow she did not feel lonely, only alone. Part of her wanted to find the path to her home. And part of her wanted to continue on the peaceful path that she had been on throughout the day.

Through the trees she could see the stars above her in the night sky. As the nocturnal animals began their waking hours, their quiet sound broke the silence of the forest. The colors had faded, but somehow Sarena was not afraid. Somehow she liked where she was in the dark and now colorless forest.

But soon it became very cold. A sharp, cold wind came suddenly from the north. She clutched her shawl around her and huddled behind a large tree. But Sarena, although cold, was not frightened.

"It is cold, but I have my shawl that I have woven out of the finest wool to keep me warm. I am alone, but I have myself to be my companion. I am far from my home, but I have carried my home within my heart."

The words that Sarena spoke surprised her, but in her heart she knew they were true.

"But I must go back to my life," she added.

"Sarena, you have not left your life. It is with you. Life is all around you. You have made your own way today. You can make your own way for the future,' again a voice spoke.

It was again very quiet except for Sarena's breathing. Sarena found some soft grass and curled up in her shawl and went to sleep. It was peaceful sleep with quiet peaceful dreams of the forest and the breeze and the stars.

Sarena awoke to a new day as it began to become light, very slowly in the forest, not with the brilliance of sunrises found in the meadows or over the sea. She still did not know the way back to her cottage, her work, the people she knew, or her dog, Samson. She wanted to find them all again.

Then she began to hear many voices, voices she recognized as people she knew. They were calling her name. She could even hear Samson barking. The voices seemed to be getting louder and soon they were no longer voices but people reaching out to her and then holding her and then crying and laughing and Samson wagging his tail and licking her face.

"We could not find you," they said. "We were frightened." "We love you." And they wre all wearing clothes made from the cloth she had woven.

Sarena hugged them. She wanted to say she was sorry, but a very soft whisper on the warm wind from the south spoke to her so that only she could hear, "Do not be sorry, Sarena. Do not be sorry."

The people led Sarena out of the forest through a beautiful meadow she had never seen before, filled with wild flowers of beautiful colors she would remember and weave into cloth someday. It was a very joyous group who proceeded down a new path to the village and Sarena's cottage. People made her warm broth and tea to drink. She felt loved and cared for.

Sarena and Samson lived many years in Sarena's cottage that she had left that day for her walk in the forest. She sometimes went back into the forest, but did not stop and continued on her path. She could return to her cottage by way of the beautiful meadow before nightfall now that she knew the way; her way.

She again wove cloth, but more beautiful than before. People continued to come by and she listened to them weave their tales as she wove their cloth. But now she knew she only had to listen, to take the stories from them and weave them into cloth for each individual; that the cloth she wove reflected her perceptions of who they were, that the cloth she wove for them could not only reflect their happiness but also their pain and sadness.

And she wove cloth for herself, a beautiful design that she took from the beauty she had found. She made the cloth into skirts for her to wear and curtains for her windows and coverings for her floors and furniture. No one else had the design that Sarena had woven for herself. Everyone knew that they could not ask for her to make it for them; that it was Sarena's.

She had been on the right path through the forest. If she had kept following her heart and her footsteps she would have found her way. But as we all know, we sometimes need others to help us along. ▦

The End

©2008 Susie Anderson

The Magic Carpet

nce upon a time there was a magic carpet with an elephant woven into the center of it with designs in reds, blues, and oranges, It arrived quite unexpectedly, and Sophie did not know where it had come from. It was rolled up tightly, wrapped in burlap and sealed with red wax. When she unwrapped it, she wondered why she had received it, where she would put it, and who she should thank. Perhaps it had come to the wrong person and she needed to find the proper owner, but her name had been on the wrapping.

She thought of all the people who could have sent it to her, but had no clue as to the real giver. She laid it on the floor and sat down on it to admire the beautiful design and colors and workmanship, when the carpet began to move ever so slightly. She thought she had accidentally moved it herself, but it again moved slowly further along the floor. She was too startled to get up off the carpet, and found that the carpet was rising to the ceiling of her cottage and was maneuvering throughout her cottage—with her hanging on for dear life!

Soon she realized that it was magical, she could not fall off the carpet, and that she was very safe. She actually began to enjoy the thrill of the ride as the carpet swooped from ceiling to floor. Then it landed on the floor next to the closed door.

She thought that perhaps the carpet wanted to go outside and fly even higher and faster, and so she opened the door. She again sat on the carpet because of its softness and the feeling of safety and comfort she felt when she was close to it. It slowly moved out the door of her cottage and began to climb into the outside air above the branches of the trees, over the rooftops, and then over the whole village.

Sophie was not in the least frightened, which greatly surprised her. She was fascinated and felt very safe. She was exhilarated with the steep turns and the feeling that she would not fall off!

Soon she and the carpet were flying away from the village, out over the hills of the surrounding countryside, toward the shore of the ocean, and then they continued out over the water. Mysteriously she felt loved and cared for and as if she were being taken on a special journey.

She usually liked to plan, be in control. She was not in control today and certainly had not planned for a mysterious journey, but that was all right. She knew somehow that she was going someplace special, although she did not know where this would be or why she was being taken there.

Sophie looked down and they were again over land. Below was a desert and a village very different from her own quiet village. This village had busy markets and many people talking rapidly and loudly. She saw a few large beautiful palaces among the smaller homes. The carpet floated to earth and landed among the booths in the market place surrounded by many people and animals including dogs, camels and even elephants.

Sophie was wearing a cotton blouse and flowered skirt with sandals on her feet. The people in this village wore silk robes and were barefoot. There were little children running throughout who wore brightly colored clothes and stopped and stared at Sophie and giggled at her strange dress and appearance.

The carpet had completely stopped moving and the whole event of the carpet landing in the market place had attracted great attention. Sophie was worried that someone would take the carpet from her, and she did not know how she would get back home without it since she did not know where she was. She was not aware of any other mode of transportation except for perhaps the camels or elephants or on foot, and that certainly would not take her across the ocean back to her home.

Sophie became frightened. She trusted the magic carpet to care for her, but if someone took it, it would not be able to take care of her, and she would be left alone in this strange place unable to let the people know her needs, since she did not know their language or they hers. She tried to stay very close to her carpet and tried to smile and look friendly in spite of feeling very frightened.

She wanted to get back on the carpet and return to the skies to swoop and soar and watch life from above and not on the ground in the midst of so many people she did not know. But the carpet just lay on the ground. She sat on it as people stared at her even more. She got up and tried to roll the carpet up and take it to a quieter place away from the crowds, but it would only lie flat and motionless upon the ground. She tried to pull it to another spot, but it would not be moved.

Soon a little boy of seven or eight years old came and gently took her by the hand and began to walk with her towards a palace close by. She did not want to go and leave her carpet, but when she looked, the carpet was following her. This caused even more stares as the people stepped out of her way.

The boy took her away from the market toward the palace. The palace was very large and made out of marble with many turrets and jewels inlaid in the sides of it. At the door was a beautiful woman who greeted Sophie and led her through the large carved wooden door. The inside was adorned with silver decorations, red velvet carpets, and velvet covered furniture.

Her carpet followed her and the boy, and soon she was led to a room with many large windows. Sophie looked at the floor, and there to her surprise was a carpet exactly like her own beloved carpet.

(Indeed her carpet had become beloved to her. It had brought her here and she had faith it would keep her safe and take her home.)

The people could not speak her language and she could not speak theirs, but there was great understanding. There were other children, beautiful little dark haired girls and boys laughing at the two carpets.

Soon Sophie's carpet waved a bit in a sort of motion for Sophie to get on it. The people motioned for her to do so also. And as she sat upon her carpet she could hear the children laughing. She turned around just as her carpet took a sharp turn out the window, to see the other carpet loaded with the children laughing and shrieking and following her and flying "in formation" as both carpets rose into the sky to the waves and cheering of the adults below.

She was charmed by the children and their smiles and laughter. Sophie was usually a quiet person. She did not laugh often. She took life very seriously. To see the children laughing made her laugh. To see their carefree abandon made her feel like one of them. She had felt safe on her carpet for some reason unknown to her and they obviously felt safe on theirs.

They again crossed above the desert, over the ocean, over the hills near her village, over the village, and then over the roof of her small cottage and landed outside her humble home. It was nothing like the palace the children had left. Sophie's village and home were quiet and there was not the noise or activity of the other village across the ocean.

The other carpet carrying the children landed by the large tree in her front yard. The children tumbled off the carpet giggling and laughing and ran to Sophie. The same little boy who had taken Sophie's hand in the village on the other side of the sea, took her hand again now.

But this time he did not lead her, but waited for her to lead him into her home. All the little children followed giggling and laughing. They were fascinated with her pottery, her lace curtains, her wooden furniture, her loom, her pots of geraniums, her pictures of her family on the walls. They made comments in their own language that she did not understand, but she knew they were as fascinated by her humble abode as she had been by their palace.

Sophie found some cookies she had made that morning and gave each some. They showed their delight and then again went outside. They petted her dog, Goliath, and some rolled on the ground with him as he sniffed and licked them and in general showed them all he liked them very much.

Then it was time for them to leave. The children hugged Sophie and tumbled back on their carpet. Sophie's carpet had now "slithered" inside her house through the open door and was lying like a normal carpet in front of her fireplace. As she looked at it the thought came to her mind, "I think my carpet is exhausted." She looked back at the laughing children waving to her as their carpet floated slowly above the trees and then swooped high above her roof and out of sight.

After the children and their carpet were gone, Sophie wanted to run and tell her friends about her experiences. This day had not been at all the way she had expected it to be. She then realized she did not know how to tell her friends of this experience, the strange appearance of the carpet, her feelings of complete safety while riding on the carpet high in the air, and the wonderful children who had then flown on a matching carpet from a far away land to her home. She knew this experience could not be shared beyond those who had also had the experience with her. But that did not matter. She felt warm and content and knew she had experienced something very special, something even perhaps spiritual.

Her carpet continued to lie before her fireplace. She placed some logs on the fire since it was getting cool as the sun went down. She wrapped her shawl around her and sat on her carpet in front of the fire and felt its softness, looked carefully at its intricate design, especially the wonderful large elephant in the very center. She looked again and it seemed to be smiling, and she thought she actually saw the elephant wink at her with the one eye she could see. She again felt warm and safe and protected.

She began to wonder if there were other carpets like hers in other faraway places for her to travel to. What would tomorrow bring? Were there other laughing children or mothers and fathers in need of an exhilarating ride with her on a matching carpet, even old men and women who no longer could travel on their own and needed a magic carpet to transport them high above the earth and life as they knew it.

The sun became faint and went down behind the hills. The stars came out and soon the moon came up in the sky. In her mind she could hear the echoes of the children's laughter as they flew out of sight. She knew they were safely back in their palace and thought about them sitting sleepily on their carpet thinking about the day as she was. She knew they were taken care of and had arrived back home safely. She believed in the magic of the carpet.

She no longer wondered where it had come from, but knew it had come from the heavens wrapped in paper and sealed with red wax for her to open and admire and take her on a wonderful ride.

A wonderful ride! Perhaps that was what life was really about, a wonderful ride on a magic carpet. Previously for Sophie the ride of her life had been through sadness. At times she had not understood the purpose or meaning of her life. She had not looked for excitement in life but settled for a mundane existence. Each day she arose, each day she endured, each day she had worked, and each day had ended in the same mundane way—until today when the carpet had arrived on her doorstep.

She felt her life now had some sort of a purpose, some spiritual, mystical meaning. The carpet had come to her, but she had willingly gone on the journey with the carpet. She had met laughing children and shown them her way of life, only briefly. She knew there would be other journeys, that there were other carpets, that there were other people for her to connect with, even for a short period of time.

Suddenly her life was filled with spirit and joy and the purpose became clear to her, to go on the journey of life, to meet people the carpet took her to meet, and to ride with these people in formation on their carpets. She looked forward to the new day, but now, she and her carpet needed to rest. 🔲

The End

©2008 Susie Anderson

The Story of the Golden Footprints

 nce upon a time there was a young woman named Sarah who lived in a village below the mountains. She was very sad and depressed. Nothing could make her happy. She had been very sad and depressed for a long time.

"What is the use of going on?" she said. Nothing anyone said seemed to make a difference.

Her best friend went to visit Sarah and told her the story of the Mountain of the Golden Footprints. "I have heard tell that at the top there is a special place. As the sun sets you can look out over the village and see sparkling golden footprints on the places where you have made a difference."

"But I haven't made a difference in anyone's life," Sarah replied. "There won't be any golden footprints for me to see. So why should I bother to go there."

"But," said her friend, "if you don't see any golden footprints, there is a special village on the other side of the mountain. That is a place for all those people who don't see any golden footprints, who haven't made a difference. They say it is comfortable and very pretty and there you can be happy. So you see there are some possibilities here. If you lived in the village on the other side of the mountain, I would miss you, but I would be glad knowing that you were once again happy. So see, you have nothing to lose."

So Sarah decided to give it a try. After all, she only wanted to be happy. She had to do something. She did not want to go on feeling the way she was. Besides, although she was pretty sure she would not see any golden footprints, she had a glimmer of hope that going there would make a difference in her life. The village on the other side of the mountain also sounded like it could be a place where she could be happy.

The next day she walked up the path to the top of the Mountain of the Golden Footprints. It was a long walk and sometimes difficult. Since she had made the decision to go to the top, she continued on, but sometimes she just wanted to stop climbing and curl up and cease to exist.

She reached the top and came to the lookout point. She was surprised to find a woman there named Faith who came and greeted her and called her by name. Faith watched over the valley below from the top of the Mountain of the Golden Footprints.

Sarah sat on a rock and looked out over her village far below. Although the sun was not setting yet, she felt inside as though she was looking out over her life. She could see her house and the house of her friend, the house of her parents, her school and many places from her childhood. She remembered many things, some sad and some happy, as she looked out over these places.

And as she was thinking about her life, the sun began to set. Lost in her thoughts, she did not really pay any attention since she did not expect to see any golden footprints. But soon a golden twinkling light began to appear on the park in the middle of the village. She still did not believe it could possibly be a golden footprint.

"Look," Faith said excitedly, "There is your first golden footprint!"

"But how could that be?" asked Sarah. "I don't remember anything I did in the park that could have possibly made a difference."

"That is my department," answered Faith. "I have watched people make golden footprints from this mountain top for many years. I remember all the golden footprint happenings."

"One day a long time ago, when you were a little child, you went laughing through the park. There was a man sitting on a bench who had just left his wife and child over a silly argument. He saw your laughter and missed his child so much that he returned to his family and lived with them happily ever after. "

"Well that was kind of accidental. I certainly didn't realize I was doing that," said Sarah. As she finished speaking, another golden sparkling footprint appeared on the house of her friend.

"Well, I did love my friend very much."

"Remember when she was very sick? You went to see her and brought her flowers and stayed with her and talked with her many hours and held her hand. If you had not done that, she would not have survived."

"But how could that be?" asked Sarah. "I'm not a doctor. I did not give her medicine. How could I have saved her life?"

"The doctor gave her good medicine, but you gave her hope. You gave her strength and courage so that her body could make the medicine work."

And as Faith finished speaking, the valley below was aglow with golden footprints. There was one on the school where Sarah's smile and love of learning had inspired a fellow student to stay in school and become a great philosopher. There was one over a tree she had planted in front of her house, and one over flowers she had planted by the side of the road.

There was one over the palace where her stubbornness had convinced the king that the village needed a smoother road for travelers, and he had smiled at her outspokenness and feisty nature.

There was a footprint right on the top of the roof of her house. That was where she had taken her children to look at the stars.

There was a golden footprint over the pub in the village where she had met her husband and they had fallen in love.

"I had forgotten all those things," said Sarah. "I was so depressed that I only remembered the sad things and not the happy things. I guess I have made a difference."

"And you will in the future," replied Faith, "There are stars to show your grandchildren and a birthday to share with your friend. And your husband needs a romantic evening at the pub."

Sarah sat for a long time until the sun had set and the golden footprints had disappeared and the lights of the village were lit in the streets and homes in the valley below and flickered, not as golden footprints, but as tiny footprints of fireflies. Soon Sarah would start down the mountain, guided by the tiny lights below.

Sarah looked all around the mountain and could see no lights except those from her village.

"Faith," she asked, "my friend told me there was a village on the other side of the mountain where people who did not see any golden footprints could go and be forever happy, but I do not see any lights except for below in my village."

"Sarah," Faith replied, "That is because no one lives there. Everyone has made golden footprints. Everyone has made a difference."

Sarah smiled and thanked Faith. She started down the mountain and knew that someday she would tell others about the Mountain of the Golden Footprints and make a difference in their lives. 🖼

The End

©2008 Susie Anderson

Michael and the Dragons

nce upon a time, Prince Michael wanted to build a castle for his new wife, Rose Blush, himself, and the children he hoped to have someday. Rose Blush was a beautiful princess. Presently they lived in the large castle of Michael's parents, the King and Queen of the kingdom. But Michael and Rose Blush, understandably, wanted their own castle.

However, every time Michael and Rose Blush found a good place for their castle, the dragons would arrive. They came to the meadow just outside the village, which would have been a good place. They came to the shores of the lake, which would have been an even more beautiful location.

Michael was very afraid of the dragons. Whenever Michael would get brave and go near them, they would roar and spit fire and throw their large spiny tails to and fro. He did not think he should fight the dragons and risk his life for the sake of a building site for a castle, but inside he felt like a coward and not as brave as a prince should be.

Finally Michael and Rose Blush found a high hill that looked out over the village, the sea, the forest, and meadows. The view was beautiful. They could see all the places that they loved. It would be the perfect place for them to build their castle. Michael was determined that the dragons would not keep him from building the castle on this site.

However, he could not forget about the dragons, although he had been up to the hill at least ten times, and the dragons had never been there. He could not understand what was keeping him from starting work on the castle. What was keeping him from standing up to the dragons anyway and confronting them?

Michael could not understand the feelings he was having. Rose Blush asked why he had not started to build the castle. He did not know what to answer her. He just said, "It's the dragons."

Now on the surface you might say, "But that isn't true. The dragons are nowhere around." But indeed it was true. It was the dragons. He was afraid they would come there. He was afraid they would come wherever he would build his castle. He felt helpless and became very depressed.

He did not feel that Rose Blush or his mother or father would understand. There were only three creatures who would understand.

And so he set off to find the dragons. He finally found them in a field just outside the village. What a sight! Three huge dragons roaring and spitting fire and throwing their tails to and fro while swarms of little yellow butterflies flew happily around them. When Michael approached, they stopped roaring, spitting fire, and throwing their spiny tails to and fro, and they sat down on the ground.

The biggest dragon, named Supreme, spoke first, "We thought you would come and find us someday."

"I'm not sure why I am here. I had to come and face you, my fears, and discover what was keeping me from building my castle," spoke Michael.

"Why are you so afraid of us?" asked Foofy, the smallest dragon.

"I am afraid you will burn me with your fiery breath, cut me with your spiny tails and. . ." Michael stopped because he could not think of any way they could have harmed him with their loud roars.

"But, Michael," said Journey, the middle-sized dragon, "We have never harmed anyone. We could, but we never have. That is just the way we live. We spit fire and roar and throw our tails to and fro."

"Well why were you always wherever I wanted to build our castle?" asked Michael.

"Well," said Foofy, "We like you. We wanted to live by you."

Michael had to think silently for a while before he spoke. Here his greatest fears liked him. "But why have you never been up to the hill where we want to build our castle?"

"Actually we thought we would wait until you built the castle, and then we would come," answered Supreme.

"I knew it! I knew you would be there someday! I knew there was a good reason I hadn't started the castle." said Michael. Then he paused, "So why don't you come now? Then I can start to build my castle."

It was a strange sight indeed—Michael skipping across the field with his greatest fears with little yellow butterflies flying around their heads, and Michael asking his greatest fears to come live by his castle! Michael was happy with his fears, the dragons.

Michael built a beautiful castle on the hill where he could see the village and the meadow and the sea, where he lived happily most of the time, with his wife, Rose Blush, his son, Ryan and his greatest fears, the dragons: Supreme, Journey, and Foofy. ▓

The End

©2008 Susie Anderson

The Moosehunter

Once upon a time, a young man and woman, Eric and Muriel, lived in a cabin by the shore of the river near a small village in the north. They were usually very happy together.

Each year during the warm season, Muriel prepared, seeded, cared for, and then harvested wonderful vegetables from her beautiful garden rimmed with lovely flowers. She worked very hard and her garden grew beautifully. What vegetables her family did not eat, she sold to others in the village and preserved others for her family's use during the winter.

Eric was a moosehunter. He also seemed to work hard as he went out early each morning and came back at night very tired. The only problem was that he never caught a moose. Now catching a moose is not an easy task, but Eric had been hunting moose for many years, and since his profession was moosehunter he was supposed to catch moose.

Eric told the men in the village all about moose. He said that they were always on the move. They did not live in herds. He said they didn't move in straight lines, but often doubled back in their journeys to check to see if they were being followed. He told them that moose ate willow buds, green leaves and water plants and sometimes a big caterpillar or other bug. In the winter they ate woody twigs of poplar, birch, alder, and willow. He even told them that moose had no upper teeth.

How did he know these things?

Eric told them how moose really couldn't see too well but had an excellent sense of smell and the big ears helped them hear the living creatures in their surroundings. He said the long legs and special hooves of the moose were the reason he never caught them as they could quickly escape. They could run through forests, rivers, swamps and over the snow in winter.

When he was not with them, the other men in the village sometimes talked about Eric. "How does he know so much about moose and yet has never been successful in his hunt for one?" they wondered. They thought this was very mysterious. They knew Eric was very smart and thought it was very mysterious he had never brought a moose home.

The townspeople had heard the moans and calls of the moose. They had sometimes glimpsed moose racks through the trees in the forests, or seen moose tracks or moose droppings near the trails. An old man in the village had even told about a moose that had come into the village one day back some twenty years ago. But no one knew as much about moose as Eric did. He was an expert on moose.

Eric would talk about the big moose he would shoot someday. This moose would make up for all the times he had not caught moose before, that one moose caught in a lifetime was a great accomplishment for a great moose hunter. One moose could feed many people all winter. The moose hide could make moccasins, blankets, and even coverings for boats. Others in the village had bagged moose and one moose had sustained them for a long time. Muriel would be able to make moose stew and other delicious moose meals.

Muriel believed in Eric and defended him when her friends would criticize him. "Why do you put up with this, Muriel? Eric has been hunting moose forever and never caught one while you are working hard growing vegetables. Maybe he needs to get a different job," they would say.

"But he is a good man," Muriel would reply. "He tries very hard. He knows more about moose than anyone in the village. He'll get one someday." As time went by she did not defend him with the assurance she had before. She began to doubt he would ever get a moose.

At first she would also think about the big moose Eric would catch someday, but since this never occurred they continued to eat vegetables. Every morning Eric would get dressed in his moose hunting clothes: his leather boots, jacket and cap, plaid shirt and green pants. He would take his rifle and go out to hunt moose. He followed moose tracks and would often tell of seeing the large antlers of a moose through the trees or over the long grass. He would come home with moose stories and tales of adventures of chasing moose, even if he didn't come home with the moose.

He would tell stories of moose with antlers eight feet wide, of them wading in the streams and marshy areas, of even seeing a moose cow with two babies. Although Muriel never admitted it to Eric, she loved the stories and was learning a great deal about moose. But still she longed to have a gorgeous moose jacket to keep her warm in the wintertime.

Muriel truly loved Eric, but began to doubt he would ever catch a moose. She believed that he actually went out with the intention of hunting and bagging the moose every day and often saw the moose. But she wondered, as friends did, why there was never the moose head above their fireplace, moose blankets on their beds or moose gloves on their fingers. Still Eric talked about hunting the moose and others listened politely, if not always attentively.

After many months of Eric hunting moose with no success, and his becoming more and more obsessed with the moose, Muriel began to feel left out of Eric's life. Each day he went on a quest with no result. It seemed to hold some secrecy and she felt lonely and a part from him. She longed for him to catch the moose so that he would be again part of her life and they could have some pursuits together.

And still each day Eric would set out along the river shore alone. He would spend all his days alone in the woods and along the marshes. He seemed to be becoming a loner, and sometimes Muriel grew tired of only talking about moose. She would try to tell him about her vegetables and ask him to come and see her garden which was doing very well. He would be polite and tell her how beautiful he thought the cabbage and beans and corn were, but still he seemed obsessed with the moose. Sometimes she thought he didn't want to hear about her vegetables because he felt guilty she was feeding their family and he was not doing his part.

One morning Eric and Muriel were eating their porridge and Muriel looked out the window… and into the dark eyes of a moose! She was so excited she could not speak. She saw his majestic rack and his beautiful dark eyes, his soft brown coat, even his eyelashes! He was that close. As soon as she could speak, she told Eric and he ran to get into his hunting clothes, but, alas, the moose had disappeared.

Muriel had never seen a moose and was amazed at his beauty, his majesty, his greatness. She could understand Eric's being drawn to the moose, his wanting to be a moosehunter and search for this beautiful animal. But when she thought of Eric actually killing this animal, bringing him home, cutting him into pieces, she was deeply saddened. She had sometimes been angry that Eric never caught a moose. She had sometimes been angry that she alone had to grow and provide the food for the family, that she worked hard with great results, while Eric, although he went out hunting through rain and snow, great heat and cold, the darkness of winter, every day of the year, had not provided for her. She now was suddenly glad Eric had never killed a moose after having looked into the eyes of this majestic animal.

Each morning the moose would appear and Muriel would look into his eyes, and he would disappear when Eric would get ready to go out to hunt him. Muriel sometimes would not even tell Eric the moose was there, but would gaze into the huge eyes of the moose and felt she was in the company of greatness. The moose would come silently, stand silently and leave silently when no one was watching. He was huge and great and Muriel looked on him with great admiration. She was not afraid. She felt she was in the presence of greatness as she gazed at him.

One morning there had been a few inches of snow. Eric thought that this time he would certainly be able to follow the moose tracks and bag the great moose. After the moose appeared outside their window, he set out to follow the tracks. Soon Muriel became gravely concerned that the huge animal she had come to love would not survive the day after many years of Eric hunting the moose. She could not stay quietly at home, and so she put on her warm clothes and set out to follow Eric's tracks, which were following the moose tracks. The tracks continued up through the hills, through the forests, down into the valley and through the marshland. The days were short as winter was approaching and soon the sun began to set.

Finally she caught up with Eric. He was sitting quietly on a log, looking through a clump of trees at the majestic moose outlined by the full moon that had risen. Eric was surprised to see Muriel, but motioned her to quietly come sit by him. He put his arm around her as the two of them watched the majesty of the moose. In some ways the moose looked out of proportion with his large horns and large head and long legs, but there was something in his eyes. She knew the moose knew they were there. She and Eric sat quietly for a long time. The air was still and there was great silence amongst the newly fallen snow. They felt like they had come to the home of the moose to stand and watch, as he had come to their home where he had stood and watched them. They felt, at a spiritual level, the greatness and power.

After a period of time Muriel began to shiver with the cold. She had been outside in the cold for a long time. Eric and Muriel got up from the log and left the moose and walked following the tracks of each of them and the moose back through the marshland and through the valley, through the forest, and up into the hills and back to their home. When they arrived it was well past midnight and Muriel fixed Eric some hot tea and bread while Eric built the fire. They ate silently, but with a great feeling of love between them.

It was a while before they spoke. Eric said, "Muriel, I have a confession for you. I have seen the moose many times. I have seen his horns through the trees, his great body walking across the river, his tracks in the snow, even his children in the marsh with their mother. I think he is the most beautiful creature I have ever known, besides you, of course, Muriel. Sometimes I feel at one with him. Sometimes I feel he leads me to the most beautiful places in the world. Sometimes he leads me through difficult places like forests and marshes. Sometimes he looks at me with his large eyes. He has taught me a great deal about himself."

"I could never shoot him, Muriel. I also could never stop being led by him,"

Eric continued, "I have seen great mountains and rivers and small animals and beautiful flowers when I have followed him. I have seen him in the cold of winter surrounded by the beauty of the northern lights. He is silent but speaks great things to me in a way I cannot explain.

"I did not think you would understand or my friends would understand. I'm sorry I have not been productive as you have. But I knew that my work was to follow the moose wherever he led me. It was a kind of quest. I learned to love him. I think, in the past weeks, he has also made you a part of this wonderful spiritual nature he and I have together. I think he somehow realized that I was leaving you out of my life. Then you found him by our window. Somehow I feel he knows great things. Somehow I feel he knows me."

Muriel answered, "I trusted you Eric. I thought you were pursuing a dream that never came about. I never got the coats and gloves and blankets from the moose that I dreamed I would have. But then the dream appeared right outside the window. You had been the hunter and I found what you had been hunting. The dream you pursued appeared to me right here where I lived and not in some far off place. I felt the majesty and beauty. As soon as I saw the moose, I realized you were led by that which you hunted."

Eric and Muriel talked long into the night.

After that night, Eric no longer pretended to be a moosehunter. He had found the moose, as had Muriel. He had found wisdom. He had found his soul. He had found his love, Muriel. Eric took Muriel and showed her all the many beautiful places the moose had taken him. They explored the forest and valleys and marshland together. At the end of the day Eric helped Muriel with her vegetables.

Eric could no longer pretend to Muriel or to the other people in the village that he was a moosehunter. He needed to find a new profession. So Eric became a teacher and taught the children much more than reading and writing. He often took them from the village school on hikes through the places where he had followed the moose. He showed the children the flowers and small animal tracks and small animals along the way and told them about the hills and valleys and streams and rivers and, most of all, he told them about the lives of moose: where they lived, what they ate, how they lived, about their children.

Muriel continued to grow vegetables. But now Eric helped her till the soil and plant the seeds and made her a wonderful wooden stand that they could sell the vegetables from by their house, and a portable stand that they could take to sell vegetables in the market.. With Eric's help, she did even better at selling her vegetables, which were large and beautiful because of her tender loving care.

And every morning, as Muriel fixed breakfast for herself and Eric, the moose appeared briefly by her window. Or did he? Or was it her memory of him, her vision of his majesty, her love for him, her belief in him? ▩

The End

Vino

The Red Convertible

It had been a long day of Christmas shopping. Sleep came quickly, but dreams were active and vivid. One gift for a friend had been a beautiful bottle of wine, but since a bed time drink of wine had seemed a good idea after a long tiring day, Sarah decided to open it and have some with her husband and buy her friend another the following day.

In the night the dream began, or was it a dream.? Sarah heard a noise in the kitchen and when going out there, she noticed a distinguished man in a tuxedo sitting on her kitchen cabinet.

"Who are you? Why are you sitting on my kitchen cabinet?" It is strange sometimes how in dreams we just don't have quite the same feelings we have as when we are awake. She did not fear this intrusion as she would have when awake.

"I'm the genie from your wine bottle."

"The genie? Aren't you supposed to be big and blue or something?

"No that's the way they do things in the movies. I am here to grant you three wishes, however."

"Three wishes? Do you think you could do something about world peace?"

"Now you sound like Miss America. You have to pick an easier wish. That one is impossible."

"Well, you are not making this easy. I'll have to think this over."

Sarah sat as the genie sampled one of the Christmas cookies she had made the previous evening. "Nice tree," commented the genie.

"Thank you. Okay how about something like my family and friends never having any difficulties in their lives."

"Nope, not possible, but close."

"Okay, how about that they will be able to handle whatever comes their way with the support of the others?"

"You've got that wish, Sarah. I'm ready for number two."

"How about my family and friends really knowing me, knowing my family and their beliefs and feelings?"

"You've got that wish, but you'll have to write about them in some books."

"I can do that."

"Now you've got one more wish. What will it be?"

"How about a red convertible? Right now. Right here."

"Can't do it."

"You seem to have a lot of restrictions on your wish lists. This is Christmas you know."

"Well, a red convertible right here would make a wreck of your kitchen."

"Okay, what about in the driveway?"

"Done."

"Just a thought. Do you really live in that bottle? It must be rather claustrophobic and there was wine in there."

"Living in a bottle was rather claustrophobic. Well, I'll be going now." The genie suddenly disappeared. She heard a car start up, and when she ran to look out, a red convertible drove out of the driveway. ▓

The End

©2008 Susie Anderson

The Story of Julia

Once upon a time there was a woman named Julia who lived in a small village in a small kingdom. She worked very hard. She had inside of her a sort of yearning to be a part of life, but she always had much work to do. She thought that was what she should do: take care of others, and be a good, responsible person. But still she felt the yearning and was not completely content.

Then one day an evil wizard came to her cottage and put a curse on her so that she worked harder and harder and never got any rest, time to enjoy life, or even take care of herself, until she was very tired and very sick. She went to see a wise man in the village to see if he could help her. Everyone looked up to him for his great wisdom and healing powers. He told her he could give her a magic potion to take the curse away.

Julia became even sicker when she took the magic potion. She could no longer work and had to rest and take care of herself. But soon she began to feel better, and something mysterious and exciting was happening to Julia! As the curse left her body, her yearning for life also emerged. Her life took on a radiance she had never known before!

The sky appeared as splendid as heaven to her. The birds sang like a symphony orchestra. Her home resembled a castle. A simple picnic tasted like a banquet dinner. Fields of wildflowers smelled like the palace rose gardens. All the things she touched felt soft like fine furs. Her family became as resplendent as royalty. Her husband appeared as handsome and charming as the prince of the kingdom. And her friends were transformed into elegant kings and queens. She laughed more often, sang beautiful songs, danced lovely dances. She loved the new life the magic potion and the wise man seemed to have brought to her. She knew from then on that she needed to take care of herself, love herself, and love life.

"And what about the future?" she asked the wise man. "Will the curse return? Will I need more of your magic? Will I live like this forever? Will I die?"

And the wise man answered, "Although I have studied long and hard and know many things, I do not know the answers to your questions. The curse may still be lurking quietly inside of you waiting to take over your life again, and it may do so, and you may die. But in the meantime, if you believe in the power of the magic, you will love life and find treasures in those around you worth more than all the gold in the kingdom! You now have the power to make the magic yourself. It is your choice, Julia. You may accept your magic for today with no promises or guarantees for the future, or you can spend today in fear that the curse will return. It is your choice, Julia."

Julia listened intently. She knew that her life would never be the same as it had been before the curse had been put on her. She felt a part of life and all the riches it had to offer. I'd like to say that Julia lived happily forever, but all I can definitely say is that Julia chose to live happily!

The End